JALEN ON THE GO

by **Dorothy H. Price** illustrated by **Shiane Salabie**

PICTURE WINDOW BOOKS
a capstone imprint

Published by Picture Window Books, an imprint of Capstone.
1710 Roe Crest Drive, North Mankato, Minnesota 56003
capstonepub.com

Copyright © 2023 by Capstone.
All rights reserved. No part of this publication may be reproduced in whole or in part, or stored in a retrieval system, or transmitted in any form or by any means, electronic, mechanical, photocopying, recording, or otherwise, without written permission of the publisher.

Library of Congress Cataloging-in-Publication Data is on file with the Library of Congress

ISBN 9781484671801 (paperback)
ISBN 9781484671818 (ebook PDF)

Summary: Seven-year-old Jalen Corey Pierce loves life in the city with his family and friends. From apartment adventures to outings at the zoo, community center, and museums, J.C. is always on the go! In this collection of four stories, follow J.C.'s adventures as he explores city life.

Designer: Tracy Davies

Design Elements:
Shutterstock: Alexzel, Betelejze, cuppuccino, wormig

Printed and bound in China. 5130

FRIENDSHIP FLOWERS 6

LAUNDRY DAY OVERLOAD 28

MUSEUM MIX-UP 50

SHARING THE MOUND 72

MEET J.C.

Hi! My name is Jalen Corey Pierce, but everyone calls me J.C. I am seven years old. I live with Mom, Dad, and my baby sister, Maya. Nana and Pop-Pop live in our apartment building too. So do my two best friends, Amir and Vicky.

My family and I used to live in a small town. Now I live in a city with big buildings and lots of people. Come along with me on all my new adventures!

FRIENDSHIP FLOWERS

Chapter 1
FLOWER FESTIVAL

Saturday was finally here!

J.C. was headed to the Spring Flower Festival with Nana, Pop-Pop, and Maya.

Nana used to be a botanist. She knew *a lot* about flowers.

J.C. was eager for Nana to teach him about the flowers at the festival.

But that was before Amir and Vicky called. They invited J.C. to the zoo.

"Nana, will we be back from the flower festival by two o'clock?" J.C. asked. "I want to go to the zoo with my friends."

"I'm sure we will, J.C.," Nana replied.

Pop-Pop tucked Maya into her baby carrier. Nana packed the diaper bag. J.C. searched high and low for Ellie the Elephant. That was Maya's favorite toy.

Soon, the four of them were on their way. But when they entered the subway, J.C. knew something was wrong.

"Why are there so many people?" he asked.

"The train must be delayed," Pop-Pop said.

J.C. was worried. If they were late, they wouldn't be back in time for the zoo!

Chapter 2
DELAYED!

A few minutes later, the train arrived. Everyone crowded on.

"Pop-Pop, what time is it now?" J.C. asked.

Pop-Pop peeked at his watch. "Almost ten o'clock," he said.

"Do you think we'll still be back in time for the zoo?" J.C. asked.

"I'm sure we will," Pop-Pop replied.

Finally, J.C. and his family arrived at the Spring Flower Festival. The smell of beautiful blooms drifted through the air. Something else drifted too.

"*Ewwww!*" J.C. said. "Maya, is that you?"

Maya giggled.

"I think somebody needs a diaper change," said Nana. She wrinkled her nose.

"We're not seeing any flowers until this little lady is cleaned up," Pop-Pop agreed. "I'll go do it."

J.C. frowned. Another delay! They'd definitely be late getting back for the zoo now.

CITY ZOO

J.C. and Nana waited for Maya and Pop-Pop. Then J.C. noticed a large sign shaped like an arrow.

"Nana, that sign says the City Zoo is that way," J.C. said.

Nana nodded. "It sure does, J.C.! I didn't realize the Spring Flower Festival moved closer to the zoo this year."

"That means we don't have to go home," J.C. said. "Amir and Vicky can meet us here. Then we can go to the zoo!"

"That's a great idea!" Nana replied. She called Amir's and Vicky's parents to tell them.

J.C. was relieved. Now he could really enjoy the Spring Flower Festival!

Pop-Pop came back with Maya. It was time to start exploring.

Nana led the way through the colorful maze. She pointed out the different flowers.

"This is a great white trillium," Nana explained.

"It has three petals," J.C. said.

"Trilliums are long-lasting flowers," Nana said. "They can live up to twenty-five years."

"Twenty-five years? That's way older than me!" J.C. exclaimed.

Chapter 4
FRIENDSHIP FLOWERS

J.C. and his family continued through the colorful maze. They were having so much fun that J.C. forgot to worry about the time.

"J.C., Amir and Vicky will be meeting you here soon to go to the zoo," Pop-Pop reminded him.

"Can I buy something before I meet up with them?" J.C. asked.

"Of course you can," Nana answered.

J.C. found what he was looking for in the gift shop. Then he went to meet his friends. He handed Amir and Vicky their gifts.

"These are for you," J.C. said. "They're called great white trilliums. They have three petals, like the three of us."

"Thanks for the beautiful flower," Vicky said.

"It smells good too," Amir replied.

J.C. smiled. He was happy that he'd found friendship flowers at the Spring Flower Festival.

"Now we're ready for the zoo!" he exclaimed.

LAUNDRY DAY OVERLOAD

Chapter 1
LAUNDRY DAY

"Can I help with laundry today?" J.C. asked Mom one Saturday morning.

J.C. and his family lived in an apartment building. They didn't have their own washer and dryer.

Instead, everyone used the building's laundry room.

"Sure," Mom replied. "We can add it to your chore list. Dad can stay with Maya. She needs a nap."

"Sounds like a plan," Dad replied. He put Maya in her crib.

"Now I have three chores," J.C. said. "Cleaning my room, dusting the bookshelves, and helping with laundry."

J.C. helped Mom carry the laundry down the hall. He pressed the button. Then they got onto the elevator.

In the laundry room, Mom sorted the clothes into piles.

"Put each pile into a different washer," she told J.C. "Each load gets one scoop of detergent."

"Got it!" J.C. replied.

Chapter 2
SUDS, SUDS, SUDS

J.C. picked up a pile of dirty clothes. He put them into the washer. Then he looked for another machine. But the rest were taken.

Mom was busy sorting laundry. J.C. didn't want to bother her.

He put the rest of the clothes into the same machine. Then he added extra detergent. That way everything would be extra clean.

J.C. closed the door. Mom came over and added the coins. Then she pressed a few buttons to start the wash.

They sat down to wait. A few minutes later, a mound of suds started coming out of the machine.

"Uh-oh," J.C. said.

"What's wrong?" asked Mom. She looked up to see suds spilling everywhere. "J.C., how much detergent did you add?"

"Four scoops," J.C. said.

Mom frowned. "That's way more than *one*, J.C."

"I put all the clothes in one machine. The rest were taken," J.C. explained. "I added extra soap to make sure *all* the clothes were clean."

"One scoop would have done the trick," Mom replied.

"I'm sorry," J.C. replied.

"We need to get this fixed, fast!" Mom told him. "We're not the only family who uses the laundry room."

"I think I know who can help!" J.C. said.

Chapter 3
HELP IS ON THE WAY!

J.C. rushed down the hall. Mr. Jackson, the maintenance man, was in his office.

"Can you please help us in the laundry room? There are suds everywhere!" J.C. exclaimed.

"Sure can, young man. Let's go!" said Mr. Jackson. He grabbed a machine with a long handle and wheels.

In the laundry room, suds were still piling up. Mom didn't look happy.

"Looks like someone used a few too many scoops of detergent, huh?" Mr. Jackson said.

"We're very sorry. It's J.C.'s first laundry day," Mom explained.

"Don't worry. This machine will suck up the suds in no time," said Mr. Jackson.

"Can I help?" J.C. asked.

"Sure," Mr. Jackson replied.

J.C. and Mr. Jackson took turns using the machine. No one could use the laundry room until they were done.

J.C. felt bad. Not following directions was *not* a good idea.

Chapter 4
EXHAUSTED

Finally, Mom and J.C. went back to their apartment. They had loads of clean clothes. But J.C.'s shoes were wet from helping Mr. Jackson.

"Laundry day sure was long," Dad said.

"We had a little laundry overload," said Mom. "But it won't happen again, right, J.C.?"

J.C. nodded. "Now I know one scoop means *one* scoop," he said. "And that if something goes wrong in the building, we're not the only ones dealing with it."

"That's right," Dad said. "It's different now that we live in an apartment instead of a house."

"I'm just glad laundry day is done," J.C. said.

"Until next week," Mom said with a wink.

MUSEUM MIX-UP

Chapter 1
CLASS TRIP

J.C. was excited to go to school. His class was going on a field trip! They were visiting the Famous Black Americans Museum.

"I can't wait for the class trip!" J.C. exclaimed.

J.C.'s dad was also going to the museum. He was an artist and excited to chaperone.

"Let's get going!" Dad said.

At school, J.C.'s teacher showed everyone a map of the museum.

"The museum might be crowded," Mrs. Rowe said. "Please stay together. I don't want anyone to get lost."

J.C. studied the map carefully. Then Mrs. Rowe split the class into groups.

"Group one will be with me," she said. "Group two will be with Mr. Pierce."

J.C. smiled at Amir and Vicky. They were all in the same group.

J.C.'s dad had been busy reading about a special new exhibit. It had wax figures of famous people.

"Oh!" he said. "Is it time? Is group two ready to rock and roll?"

"Yes!" they replied.

Chapter 2
FAMOUS FACES

Mrs. Rowe led the way to the subway. Everyone squeezed onto the train.

A few stops later, they reached the museum. The entrance was packed!

"I need to use the bathroom," Amir said.

"Mrs. Rowe, you can get started. We'll catch up," Dad said.

Group one started their tour. Amir went to the bathroom. Then Dad led the group toward the exhibit.

Each wax figure had a sign in front of it. The sign explained why the person was famous.

"That's Madam C.J. Walker," J.C. read.

"She was a very successful businesswoman," Dad explained.

"This one is Matthew Henson," Amir said.

"He was a great explorer," Dad told them. "And the first Black American to visit the North Pole."

"Over there!" Vicky pointed. "That's Kamala Harris."

"She is our first female vice president," Dad said. "She's also our first Black and Indian vice president."

"They all look so real!" Vicky added.

"They sure do," Dad agreed.

They reached the end of the first room. The hallway split in two directions. There were people *everywhere.*

"I don't see Mrs. Rowe or group one," Vicky said. She looked worried.

"Me neither," Amir added.

Dad looked worried too. "I'm all mixed up," he said. "Which way should we go?"

Chapter 3
PAYING ATTENTION

J.C. thought back to that morning at school. "I know!" he said. "We should go right."

"Are you sure?" Dad asked.

Vicky nodded. "Mrs. Rowe showed us the museum map in case we got lost."

"J.C. is right," said Amir. "Right is right."

"I guess I should have listened more carefully," Dad said. "I'm glad you all paid attention!"

Group two kept right and continued the tour. They saw figures of Cicely Tyson, Maya Angelou, and Barack Obama.

They passed lots of other classes and groups. But they didn't see group one. Finally . . .

"There they are!" J.C. pointed.

Dad and group two walked fast to catch up.

"You finally found us," said Mrs. Rowe.

"Thanks to my group," Dad said. "They remembered the museum map you showed us."

"It's good to know everyone paid attention," Mrs. Rowe replied.

Chapter 4
SOUVENIRS

The groups stayed close together for the rest of the tour. There were no more mix-ups.

When it was over, everyone stopped in the museum gift shop.

"Does anyone want to buy a souvenir?" Mrs. Rowe asked.

"I like this Madam C.J. Walker key chain. I want to be successful like her," J.C. said.

"This Matthew Henson snow globe is cool. I want to visit the North Pole one day," Amir said.

"I'll buy this Kamala Harris pin," Vicky said. "I want to be vice president when I grow up. And then president!"

"Those are wonderful ideas," Dad replied.

"Let's thank Mr. Pierce for chaperoning our class trip," said Mrs. Rowe.

"Thank you, Mr. Pierce!" the class said.

Dad laughed. "You're all welcome. Now, who knows how to get home?"

SHARING THE MOUND

Chapter 1
PLAY BALL

J.C. loved going to the community center near his family's apartment building. This week, he saw a special flyer. The center was going to have a baseball team!

Baseball was J.C.'s favorite sport. He used to play in his old town. He already had a bat, a glove, a helmet, and cleats. That was everything he needed.

J.C. told Amir and Vicky.
They wanted to play too.

On Saturday, everyone met at the city field. The coach split the group into teams. Vicky, Amir, and J.C. were on the same team.

"The game will have six innings," Coach Zach explained. "Team one will bat first. After three outs, we'll switch. Ready to play ball?"

"Yes!" everyone replied.

J.C.'s team took the field first.

J.C. really wanted to pitch.

"I was the best pitcher on my old team," he told the coach.

"Vicky is going to pitch first," Coach Zach said. "But everyone will switch positions. You're at second base to start."

J.C. frowned. He was ready to show off his skills. But he did what Coach said and went to his base.

Chapter 2
STRIKE THREE

Vicky threw the first pitch.

The batter struck out.

The next batter hit a fly ball. Amir caught it at third base.

The third batter hit the ball to second base. J.C. caught it.

That was three outs! J.C.'s team was up to bat.

"You can bat first," Amir offered.

"Thanks! I was the best batter on my old team," J.C. said.

J.C. stepped up to the plate.

All eyes were on him.

The pitcher threw the ball. J.C. swung, but he missed. Strike one.

J.C. took a deep breath. The pitcher threw the next ball. J.C. missed that pitch too. Strike two.

J.C. had one more chance. He swung for the third pitch, but he missed—again.

"Strike three," Coach Zach said. "J.C., you're out."

Chapter 3
HAVING FUN

J.C. felt down. He didn't get to pitch. And he had struck out. Baseball was not very fun.

"It's okay, J.C.," Vicky said.

"You'll get a hit next time," Amir added.

"I hope so," J.C. said.

Amir and Vicky batted next. They both hit the ball. Amir got out at third base. Vicky scored a run.

The next batter struck out. That was three outs. That meant J.C.'s team was back on the field.

"J.C., your turn to pitch," said Coach Zach. "Let's see what you can do."

J.C. went to the mound.

"Come on, J.C.!" his teammates cheered. "You can do it!"

J.C. took a deep breath.

Everyone else was having fun.

He decided to have fun too.

J.C. threw the first pitch.

The ball flew over the plate.

"Strike one!" Coach called.

J.C. threw the second pitch.

The batter swung and missed.

"Strike two!" Coach called.

J.C. threw the third pitch.

"Strike three!" Coach Zach exclaimed. "You've got a great arm, J.C.!"

J.C. grinned. "Thanks, Coach! That was fun!"

Chapter 4
HOME RUN

A few innings passed. The game was tied. It was J.C.'s turn to hit.

The pitcher threw the first pitch. J.C. didn't swing his bat.

"Strike one," Coach called.

The pitcher threw the second pitch. J.C. swung his bat and missed.

"Strike two," Coach called.

"You can do it, J.C.!" Vicky hollered.

"Hit it out of the park!" said Amir.

Hearing his friends helped. The pitcher threw the third pitch. J.C. swung.

Pop! J.C.'s hit went way out to left field.

"Home run!" Coach Zach yelled.

J.C. ran around the bases. He grinned as he crossed home plate. His hit won the game.

"I knew you could do it, J.C." Vicky said.

"That was a great game!" Amir added. "Your home run was the best part."

"Playing *together* was the best part," J.C. said. "Thanks for making baseball fun."

LET'S TALK

1. J.C. was excited about the Spring Flower Festival, but he also wanted to go to the zoo with Amir and Vicky. Have you ever had to choose between two things you wanted to do? How did you decide?

2. J.C. wanted to help with laundry day, but he didn't listen to directions. Have you ever offered to help someone, but made a few mistakes along the way? How did you make things right?

3. There were many famous Black Americans in the wax exhibit at the museum J.C. visited. With your friends or family, talk about some other famous Black Americans J.C.'s class might have seen during the tour.

4. J.C. wasn't happy when Coach Zach let Vicky pitch first. Have you ever had to wait your turn or play a position you didn't like? What did you do?

LET'S WRITE

1. Different flowers grow in different parts of the world. Do some research to find the types of flowers that grow where you live. Describe them in a paragraph, or draw a picture!

2. Think about a time someone helped you in a tough situation. Write a thank-you note to that person. Have a grown-up help you mail it or send it by email.

3. The famous Black Americans at the museum inspired J.C. and his friends to think about what they want to do in the future. Think about the accomplishments mentioned in the story. Then make a list of things you would like to do when you grow up.

4. J.C. felt bad when he struck out, but Amir and Vicky still rooted for him. Think of a time when you felt down and your friends cheered you on. Draw a cartoon panel of that memory.

ABOUT THE CREATORS

Dorothy H. Price loves writing stories for young readers, starting with her first picture book, *Nana's Favorite Things*. A 2019 winner of the We Need Diverse Books Mentorship Program, Dorothy is also an active member of the SCBWI Carolinas. She hopes all young readers know they can grow up to write stories too.

Shiane Salabie is a Jamaica-born illustrator based in the Philadelphia tri-state area. When she moved to the United States, she discovered her first true love: the library. Shiane later realized that she wanted to bring stories to life, and now she uses her art to do so.